WONDERFUL STORIES

FOR AMAZING GIRLS

A COLLECTION OF STORIES ABOUT COURAGE,
CONFIDENCE AND FRIENDSHIP

Kianna Molly

Inspiring Stories for Amazing Girls
Kianna Molly
1st edition 2022

Content

Introduction

Good day! Do you realize how unique you are? In this world, there are countless girls, but there is only one of you. You are totally original and unique. Always keep that in mind!

You will face both big and small obstacles in this universe. You could feel like you can't succeed at times. Your level of fear or self-doubt may increase. But I'll let you in on a little secret. Everybody occasionally experiences this! even grownups. There is no such thing as a problem-free life. There is always bad when there is good.

Your life includes everything, even the things that terrify you or that you would prefer not to do.

Sometimes, negative situations can also teach us positive lessons.

The stories in this book introduce you to a lot of girls.Girls who initially lacked confidence but then bravely overcame their anxieties. Girls who struggled with self-doubt but afterwards displayed courage. Girls who were on the verge of giving up but kept on after finding their confidence. You can accomplish all of this, I'm positive. But you must begin to have confidence in yourself.

You can do that with the aid of these tales.

After each story, there will be a picture with a significant message. You are welcome to color the image. It is recommended to use a lot of vibrant hues. By doing this, you will be more likely to retain the messages and never forget them, even at the most trying times in your life.

MORAL OF THE STORY :

ALWAYS KEEP IN MIND HOW SPECIAL, LOVABLE,
AND SIGNIFICANT YOU ARE TO THIS WORLD.

EVERYTHING ABOUT YOU IS PERFECT AS IT IS!

I AM
UNIQUE

THERE IS BEAUTY IN IMPERFECTION

Once upon a time, long ago, there was a well-known Zen Temple. In that temple, there was a Lovely garden with all a variety of trees, shrubs and plants.

One of the temple's priests has a passion for gardening. So, consequently, that priest was chosen to look after the garden in the temple by the others. The priest was overjoyed with this choice and made great efforts to ensure the garden is attractive and beautiful.

Every day, without fail the priest would go to the garden. He raked the soil and took care of the garden.

Besides the temple, there was a much smaller temple. And there lived an old Zen monk. Whenever the priest came to tend to the garden, the old monk observed the priest.

One day, the priest was expecting some special guests. These guests were to arrive at the temple. So that day,

the priest took extra care of the garden. With extreme precision, he cut the grass, the shrubs and with the same precision, he raked the soil in the garden and trimmed the trees.

When raking the autumnal leaves, he took even greater care. The leaves were neatly piled up by the priest.

The garden now appeared flawless. Nothing was out of place. When he was done, he admired his hard work. He then called out to the old monk, "Doesn't this look magnificent"

"Yes, it is beautiful," agreed the old monk. "But there is one thing that you missed out. I'll set it right for you" The old monk walked across the garden to the tree and gave the trunk a mighty shake. Many leaves fell down. "Now it looks magnificent" announced the old monk.

That's when the priest realized that a little imperfection is required in things to make them look beautiful.

A total perfection is mechanical and unnatural. He remembered his lesson for the rest of his life.

MORAL OF THE STORY: IMPERFECTION MAKES US BEAUTIFUL AND MORE HUMAN.

"BE CONFIDENT WITH YOUR IMPERFECTIONS"

I AM
CONFIDENT

THE MOTHER AND HER INTELLIGENT DAUGHTER

Once upon a time, there lived a mother and a daughter together. They were extremely wealthy. Whatever her daughter demanded, the mother would get for her without any hitch.

The mother desired that her daughter value everything he had and respect everyone, regardless of caste, religion, or color.

One day, the mother decided to take her spoilt daughter on a trip.

She took her daughter to a nearby village.
She wanted to demonstrate to her the depths of poverty.

They spent time on a poor family's farm.
The girl treated the poor people very nicely and with kindness. Her mother was very surprised at her behavior.

On their return from the trip, the mother asked her daughter, "How was the trip, son?"

"It was great, mom!" the daughter replied. "What did you learn from our trip?" her mother asked.

The daughter answered, "We have one dog, they have four! We have a pool at our home but they have a huge river! We buy food for ourselves and they grow the food!"

The daughter continued, "We have so many lights at our house but they have beautiful stars!

We have walls to protect us but they have friends! All of us have television to pass our time but they have family to spend the quality time.

We have lots of money with us but they have the god with them!"
The girl's mother was speechless while her daughter was talking and realized that her daughter had noticed so well.

Then, her daughter added, "Thank you, mother for showing me how poor we are!"

MORAL OF THE STORY:

MONEY IS IMPORTANT BUT IT'S NOT ALWAYS ABOUT THE MONEY THAT MAKES US RICH, IT'S SIMPLICITY, LOVE, COMPASSION, FRIENDSHIPS, VALUES, FAMILY AND OUR
RELATIONSHIP TO GOD THAT MAKES OUR LIVES RICH.

I AM RICH
AND HAPPY

THE HARD WORK LEADS TO SUCCESS

The school's Sports Day was quickly approaching. The kids were all very excited and practicing for the big race.

Sophia, one of the school's fastest runners, was confident that she would win despite the fact that she was doing nothing only watching TV.

"To finish first in the race, you must put in a lot of effort, Sophia. You are not practicing in any way" said Sophia's mother.

Mom, you know how fast I am! Then why should I waste my time running? Only I will win, no one else will win!" exclaimed Sophia.

"Sophia, you may be right but talent without hard work is not good at all. This laziness of yours will cost you greatly" her mother warned her.

Sophia just laughed and shrugged her shoulders. she was so confident that she would win the trophy as no one else in her class was as fast as she was!

"HA HA" HA,

Sophia's classmate Isabella was also competing in the running race. she wasn't a quick runner. she was, however, very dedicated and practiced until late at night, developing great endurance and willpower to run the race.

There were only a few days until Sports Day, but Sophia did not practice at all.

Isabella, on the other hand, practiced all hours of the day and night.

The sports day was approaching, but Sophia was confident that no one could beat her and had not practiced at all. Isabella, on the other hand, had become a very fast runner thanks to her dedication and hard work.

The Sports Day had finally arrived. All of the students gathered on the field to cheer on their favorite players. The participants were given the signal to begin the race. When the coach blew the whistle, everyone took off running toward the finish line. It was thrilling. All of the racers were far behind Sophia and Isabella. They were both neck to neck.

Suddenly, Sophia outpaced Isabella. The audience applauded her. Sophia was quickly on her way to defeating Isabella.

However, when they were only a few meters away from the finish line, Isabella unexpectedly took off and ran ahead of Sophia, crossing the finish line first. Isabella's brilliant performance astounded everyone.

She accepted the trophy and the prize money with pride.

Sophia's mother approached Isabella and praised her for his efforts, saying, "You deserve it for your dedication and effort!"

"Thank you, Miss!" Isabella smiled broadly and walked happily with her trophy.

Sophia bowed her head in shame. her mother approached her and said, "Look, talent without hard work is meaningless.

That young girl worked hard and was rewarded for it. Only hard work can lead to success!"

Sophia now understood the value of hard work. This incident caused a significant shift in her life.

MORAL OF THE STORY:

TALENT IS A GREAT GIFT BUT NOTHING CAN BE ACHIEVED WITHOUT HARD WORK.

I AM SUCCESSFUL

SHAKE OFF ALL YOUR PROBLEMS

Once upon a time, there lived a man.

This man had a large number of donkeys to assist him with his business.

There was an old donkey among them.

This old donkey had been with the merchant for quite some time. As a result, the merchant had grown fond of his donkey.

One day, The old donkey fell into an open pit while the merchant and his donkeys were returning from a trip.

The donkey began to weep and cry. "Oh no," the merchant exclaimed.

"I'm not even sure I have a rope. "How should I proceed now?" " The merchant looked around for assistance.

However, the man was unable to locate anything that would assist him in bringing the donkey out.

Finally, the man decided to fill the pit.

"I should bury the donkey here because he is nearing the end of his life. And this pit, too, must be filled. I can do both things at the same time!

"The man pondered. So he went to get a shovel. The man started digging in the ground. He was working very hard.

Throughout this time, the donkey cried and wailed.

The man continued to throw dirt into the pit as he dug the ground. The donkey's wails eventually stopped.

When the man came to a stop for a short rest, what he saw surprised him. "Oh, my poor donkey. You did not give up!" The man noticed that when he threw dirt on the donkey, the donkey shook it off. As a result, dirt began to accumulate on the ground.

The donkey stepped on the now elevated ground when there was enough dirt on the ground.

The man continued to throw dirt into the pit, and the donkey kept shaking it off and rising. Finally, the donkey was rescued from the pit.

MORAL OF THE STORY :

JUST AS THE DONKEY SHOOK OFF ALL THE DIRT AND FOUND HIS WAY OUT OF THE PIT ON HIS OWN, WE TOO SHOULD TREAT OUR PROBLEMS AS THE DIRT.

ONLY AFTER SHAKING THEM OFF, WE CAN TACKLE OUR PROBLEMS!

I AM
CAPABLE

THE YOUNG CLEVER KING

Once upon a time, in the distant past, there reigned a young king.

He was both wealthy and inquisitive. Out of curiosity, the king left his palace and went to the passage outside his city one day. There, on a busy street, he decides to put his own people to the test. The king erects a massive boulder in the middle of the road. He then fled and hid in the nearby shrubs. "This should be interesting," he muffles.

From his vantage point, the young king observes a large number of people.

The first visitor was a wealthy merchant. He exclaimed loudly when he saw the massive boulder in the middle of the road, "What is the king up to? Isn't he supposed to keep these roads in good condition?"

As a result, the wealthy merchant and his men went around the massive boulder.

The young king was taken aback. "How unexpected," he reflected. Many men came after that. They all blamed the king, and some yelled. But none of them were able to move the boulder. Then a peasant arrived with a load of vegetables.

He comes to a halt when he sees the boulder in the middle of the road. The king looks at the peasant, intently watching his every move from that point forward.

Surprising the king, the peasant dropped his load of vegetables and began pushing the boulder.

After much sweating and pushing, the peasant succeeds. The peasant then begins to gather his belongings.

While he was doing so, he noticed a purse on the ground. "A purse?" he wondered. The peasant was perplexed as to where it came from.

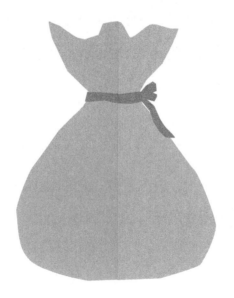

When the peasant looks closer, he discovers a note from the young king stuck to the purse that reads, "Whoever removes the boulder from the road, this is a gift to them."

The peasant discovered many gold coins inside the purse and learned a valuable lesson that many people missed. "Every obstacle provides an opportunity to improve our situation," the peasant says as he walks away with a purse full of gold coins.

MORAL OF THE STORY :

FIXING OUR OWN PROBLEMS IS FAR PREFERABLE TO BLAMING OTHERS. EVERY OBSTACLE PROVIDES AN OPPORTUNITY TO IMPROVE OUR SITUATION, AND HARD WORK ALWAYS PAYS OFF.

I AM
RESPONSIBLE

TWO GIRLS CLIMBING THE TREE

Once upon a time, there was a girl named Evelyn who enjoyed going on adventures.

She was only eight years old at the time. She was playing in the park one day. she was climbing the trees. She was an excellent climber and soon found herself thirty feet up in a tree.

Excited, She began swinging back and forth from one of its branches. She was having so much fun that she didn't notice that one of the branches could snap.

Her cousin Luna, who was just a year older started playing on the same tree.

Evelyn's father and Luna's mother noticed that the children were perched too high and could fall.

Before they could reach them, a gust of wind blew over the tree, causing it to sway.

Evelyn could hear her father's voice saying, "Evelyn, hold on tight!" Luna's mother yelled, "Luna, DON'T FALL!" Luna fell out of the tree seconds later.

Her mother rushed to her aid, but she was unharmed. Evelyn carefully scampered down the tree to safety.

When Luna's mother returned home, she inquired of Evelyn's father, "I wonder why both of our girls were hanging from the same tree, yet my older daughter fell and yours did not?"

He replied "I can't say for sure, but when the gust of wind came, you panicked and yelled, 'Luna, don't fall,' and then she did."

Luna's mother looked surprised, so Evelyn's dad explained further.

"You see, the mind processes commands.
It has a very difficult time processing fear and negativity. In order for Luna to respond to the command of not falling, she first had to imagine falling and then try to tell brain not to fall.

When Evelyn was told to hold on tightly, her brain had an instant image and command of hanging on tightly and so she did!"

Luna's mother was taken aback by his response and went home that night still thinking about what had occurred.

She believed in positive thinking, but she never considered the real-life implications and their impact on the mind and our experiences.

Moral OF THE STORY :

POSITIVE THOUGHTS AND WORDS CAN AFFECT THE OUTCOME OF OUR EXPERIENCES.

I AM
POSITIVE

MAYBE

Once upon a time, in a faraway land, there lived a farmer.

This farmer possessed vast lands. She worked in her fields all hours of the day and night. She got up early every morning and went to work. She returned home after a long day of hard work. She had a horse in his fields.

One day, the horse run away. The farmer wasn't particularly sad.

"I'm sorry to hear about your horse. It's really unfortunate, one of the farmer's neighbors said, trying to confort her.

But the farmer remained calm and said, "Who knows? Maybe"

The horse reappeared the following morning. He also brought three other wild horses with him.

The neighbors were overjoyed when they saw this. But the farmer remained calm. "How wonderful," the neighbors exclaimed, telling the farmer that everything was fine and that he now had four horses.

"Maybe," the farmer said again. All of this had no effect on her.

The farmer's son then attempted to ride one of the horses the next day.

However, he failed and broke his leg. The neighbors found out about it. "How unfortunate" they said. "Maybe" replied the farmer, still unwavering.

The following day, the army officials arrived in their village to recruit young soldiers for the war.

And the farmer's son was not drafted because he had broken his leg. The neighbors were overjoyed. They also congratulated the farmer. "Maybe," she said again.

The farmer, you see, knew that nothing was good or bad.

And that she couldn't decide whether something was good or bad because of how it ended.

As a result, she lived a happy and peaceful life.

MORAL OF THE STORY:

WHAT IS GOOD TODAY MAY NOT BE GOOD TOMORROW AND WHAT IS BAD TODAY MAY NOT BE BAD TOMORROW.

I AM
POSITIVE

ERASER AND PENCIL

Once upon a time, a pencil and an eraser were discussing each other's jobs.

They were both complimenting each other on their efforts. They both understood that they are nothing without one another.

Soon, the pencil began to draw a straight line. The eraser was watching the pencil. The pencil suddenly lost its balance, and the straight line it had created was ruined.

The pencil became very sad because she realized the eraser would have to suffer as a result of her error.

The pencil said to eraser, "I am so sorry!" The eraser did not know what pencil was talking about so it asked, "For what my dear friend?"

"I am sorry, you get hurt because of me.

You are always there to correct any mistakes I make.

But each time you erase my mistakes, you lose a piece of yourself and grow smaller, "cried the pencil.

When the eraser heard this, he said, "That is correct, but I don't mind.

You see, I was made to do this, to assist you whenever you made a mistake. Even though I know I'll be gone one day. I'm actually pleased with my job. So, please, don't be concerned! If I see you sad, I will not be happy."

Reflection through the story: Our parents are just like eraser, and we are the pencil.

They are always present for their children, cleaning up after them. They are sometimes hurt along the way, and as time passes, they grow older and older.

The parents are always happy with what they do for their children and will always hate seeing their precious ones worrying or sad.

MORAL OF THE STORY :

TAKE CARE OF YOUR PARENTS, TREAT THEM WITH KINDNESS. AND MOST IMPORTANTLY LOVE THEM THE MOST.

I AM AN AMAZING PERSON

SMALL THINGS MATTERS

It was a gorgeous Sunday morning on the beach.

The sun was shining brightly, and the air was crisp. But, in addition to the morning tides, there were hundreds of starfish on the beach.

They couldn't get back into the ocean and the sun was rising so quickly. These starfish would perish.

On the beach, there was a little girl building a sandcastle and playing alone. she was overjoyed over there.

She wouldn't notice the starfishes at first. But later, when she lost concentration while building the castle, she noticed something on the beach.

As she looked around, she noticed a lot of starfish laying around, almost waiting to die.

She thought for a while and quickly realized what she needed to do.

So she got up and stood there. She paused for a moment and thought to herself, "Yes, I can help them!

I should help them! But how exactly?"
There were hundreds of starfishes on the ground, and it was impossible for her to save each one by returning them to the ocean.

But, without wasting any time, she began moving towards all of those starfishes and then began taking them one by one in her hand and returning them to the ocean.

She did it several times for dozens of starfish over there.

She was aware that there were an increasing number of starfishes waiting for her, but she did not stop.

She kept dropping those starfishes into the water one by one, carrying them in his hand.

Her father stood some distance away, watching her.

He couldn't figure out what his daughter was up to.

So he inquired, "What exactly are you doing? There are a lot of starfish! How many of them can you assist? What difference does it really make?"

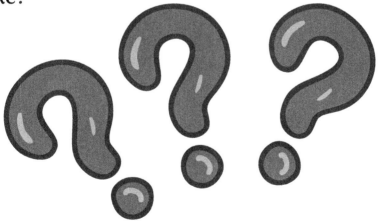

But his daughter only smiled as she thrown another starfish into the water, saying, "It makes a difference for at least this starfish, if not others, father!"

His father was really surprised and shocked by his daughter's answer.

But at the same time, he was really happy for his daughter.

MORAL OF THE STORY :

IT DOES NOT MATTER IF WE ARE MAKING A BIG
OR SMALL DIFFERENCE.

BECAUSE ONCE EVERYONE STARTS MAKING A
SMALL DIFFERENCE, IT'S GOING TO BE THE BIG
DIFFERENCE.

I AM
ENOUGH

YOU BECOME WHAT YOU BELIEVE

Once upon a time, an eagle lived on the mountainside.

In its nest, the eagle had laid four large eggs. Then there was a massive earthquake one day.

One of the four eggs rolled down the valley into a chicken farm as the earth shook.

When the chickens discovered the enormous egg, they decided to guard it.

They treated it the same way they would their own eggs.

The eagle's egg eventually hatched alongside the others. The chickens were just chickens at this point, with no knowledge of eagles or their young.

As a result, the eaglet was treated and raised like a chicken.

The eaglet was looking up at the sky one day.

And an eagle soaring in the sky piqued his interest.

So the eaglet tells his chicken friends that he, too, aspires to soar like the eagle.

He was mocked by the other chickens. ""You?" they mocked, "you are no eagle!" You, like the rest of us, are a chicken. Furthermore, chickens do not fly!"

The baby eagle was satisfied with his chicken family, but something seemed to be missing.

Every day, the baby eagle would gaze up at the sky and wish he could fly.

And every time he expressed his desire to fly, he was told, "You cannot fly, you are a chicken, and that is all you will ever be!"

As the chickens grew older, they began to imitate their mother. The baby chicks began to walk and eat like her.

And the poor eagle was forced to do the same. The chicks matured into chickens over time. And the eaglet grew into an eagle as well.

The eagle eventually stopped fantasizing about flying in the open skies. In addition, the eagle stopped talking about it.

As time passed, the eagle began to behave more like a chicken and less like an eagle. And he died like a chicken without discovering his full potential.

MORAL OF THE STORY:

YOU BECOME WHAT YOU BELIEVE.

DARE TO DREAM AND DARE TO FOLLOW IT.

I AM A DREAMER

THE ANT AND THE DOVE

On a steamy day, an ant was strolling along the riverbank.

The poor ant fell into the water after losing her balance. "Please help me! help me! "The ant screamed.

She cried out in pain. She was dragged away by the river's powerful flow. She screamed, "Someone, please help me!"

A bird was observing everything from a tree close by. In the water, the ant was fighting for its life. The small ant made the dove very sad.

The ant was constantly begging for help. The dove thought, "Oh no, the little ant is in danger. The dove chose to rescue the ant.

Ant heard him say, "Be at rest, my friend! I'll make sure you're safe!"

The dove quickly tore a leaf off and threw it into the water next to the ant that was battling. The ant approached the leaf and climbed it.

The ant safely reached the coast. I will always be grateful to you for saving my life, the thankful ant said.

Few weeks later, the ant saw a bad hunter with the gun. The hunter was targeting at the dove sitting on the tree.

Guessing what he was about to do, the ant quickly bit him on the heel. "Ouch! You pathetic ant!

What have you done?" the hunter yelled. The ant walked away happily as she was able to help the dove in return.

MORAL OF THE STORY:

EVERY GOOD DEED WE DO FOR OTHERS WILL SURELY COME BACK TO US.

I AM A HELPFUL PERSON

AN HONEST GIRL

Once, there was a very poor girl named Olivia. She lived with her family. her parents worked hard to raise their daughter.

Olivia was a very good girl and always spoke the truth.

Her parents taught her that "Honesty is the best policy!"

Olivia's small village was visited by the King one day, and everyone came out to welcome him.

The King was distributing candy and cookies. The peasants gathered close to the King's carriage in an effort to grab some of his gifts.

When the King finally reached Olivia, he gifted her with a box of cookies and candies.

Olivia was so happy that she went home to give the chocolates to her family right away.

When Olivia got back to her house, she saw a lovely ring among the sweets.

She thought to herself that this ring could make her rich. And she and her family no longer had to worry about having enough food to eat.

After thinking about what to do all the day, Olivia decided to return the ring to the King.

Olivia went to the palace and returned the King's ring.

The King was very thankful to Olivia and said to her, "this is my favorite ring!"

You are a very honest girl and I want to reward you with lots and lots of gold coins!" When Olivia's parents got to know about her honesty, they became very happy.

When Olivia came home, her parents hugged her. From that day, Olivia was a very rich girl and her family never went hungry again.

MORAL OF THE STORY :

Always Be Honest with others and with yourself.

I AM A HONEST PERSON

I AM AN AMAZING PERSON

Printed in Great Britain
by Amazon